THE BEASTS

CINEMATIC GUIDE

SCHOLASTIC INC.

Cover: background: © Renzzo/Dreamstime

By Felicity Baker
Art Direction: Rick DeMonico
Page Design: Heather Barber

CONTENTS

INTRODUCTION

Fantastic Beasts and Where to Find Them™ is the story of the wizard Newt Scamander and his adventures with his beasts.

When more than a few magical creatures escape from his case, Newt must go on a chase throughout New York City to retrieve them—which soon turns into an epic adventure!

Magizoology is the study of magical creatures: the fantastic beasts who are part of the wizarding world, outside of No-Maj awareness.

Currently, there is only one known Magizoologist: Newt Scamander. Newt feels more comfortable around beasts than he does around humans.

Newt is working on a manuscript entitled *Fantastic Beasts and Where to Find Them* to educate the wizarding community about the beauty and importance of magical creatures.

Newton ("Newt") Artemis Fido Scamander
has a mission: to find and study all the fantastic
beasts in existence, either in their natural
habitats or in ones he re-creates in his case.

Newt attended Hogwarts School of Witchcraft and Wizardry where
he was sorted into Hufflepuff house. While a student at Hogwarts,
Newt was caught up in an unfortunate incident in which he took
the blame for another student's life-endangering mistake. Despite
Professor Dumbledore's pleas, Newt was still expelled.

"WHAT MAKES ALBUS DUMBLEDORE SO FOND OF YOU, MR. SCAMANDER?"

-PERCIVAL GRAVES

When the Great War raged, Newt worked with the Ministry of Magic on a classified program to wrangle dragons. He commanded Ukranian Ironbellies, but the Ministry canceled the program because the unruly dragons tried to devour everyone *but* Newt. After the war ended, Newt ventured across the globe to write a book on Magizoology that would serve as both a record of his observations and as a learning tool for others.

NEWT'S CASE

To protect the beasts he finds, some of which are endangered, Newt provides habitats called biomes for them inside his leather case—however unbelievable that may seem!

On the outside, Newt's brown case looks like it could be purchased at any leather goods store. In fact, Newt's adventure in New York City begins *because* of how ordinary his case looks.

While at Steen National Bank, Newt meets Jacob Kowalski, a person without any magical abilities, which in America is called a No-Maj. Jacob accidentally takes Newt's case thinking it is his own!

The thing that sets Newt's case apart is that it has two different modes, activated by switching a special lock. In the first mode, "Muggle Worthy," the case opens to reveal various personal effects. In the second mode, the brass dial on the lock can be rotated to "Open." This transforms Newt's case into a pathway to a wholly magical environment where he keeps and cares for dozens of fantastic beasts.

Inside the world of the case, each creature lives in its own special habitat.

The beasts are comfortable inside the case, free from the worry of starvation or extermination. Nonetheless, when Newt's magical lock becomes momentarily faulty, the Niffler, an especially curious beast, slips out.

"DON'T PANIC. THERE'S ABSOLUTELY NOTHING TO WORRY ABOUT."

-NEWT SCAMANDER

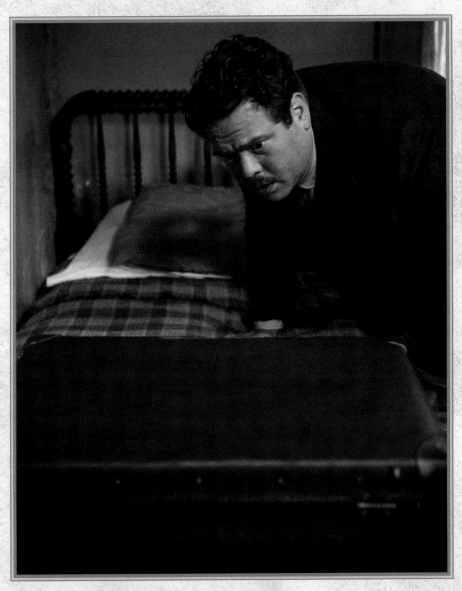

When Jacob later gets home and opens up Newt's case, he unwittingly releases many of the remaining beasts, exposing New York City to chaos. Jacob even gets a nasty bite on his neck from an escaping Murtlap.

In addition to containing the beasts' habitats, the case is also home to Newt's private shed.

The shed stores everything necessary to maintain the health and well-being of Newt's beasts.

Newt also keeps equipment in his shed that he might need during his outings to catch magical creatures. There is also a typewriter onto which Newt types the pages of his book.

Newt has stockpiled crates of food pellets and carefully arranged bottles such as Shell Shiner, Beak Balm, Feather Floss, Hoof Healer Ointment, and more.

Newt also keeps charts about each beast's feeding and habitat needs.

Part of the shed's interior has been turned into a laboratory. Beakers and jars containing herbs and other ingredients can be found on Newt's desk and shelves.

Newt uses these ingredients to concoct his magical potions, and mixes the salves that help him care for his beasts.

THE BEASTS

From charming little beasts that can fit into Newt's pocket to terrifying giants that can blast holes into brick walls, Newt's case is a safe haven for all beasts. Whether they are cuddly or inspire fear, Newt loves and cares for them all equally.

BILLYWIG

A Billywig can zip through the air so quickly that Newt needs to zap one with his wand to catch it. The outside of its body is a brilliant blue, the color of sapphires.

This Billywig soars in the sky just above a crowd of New Yorkers. The No-Majs are oblivious, but not Tina Goldstein, a witch.

"WE'RE GOING TO RECAPTURE MY
CREATURES BEFORE THEY GET HURT.
THEY ARE CURRENTLY IN ALIEN
TERRAIN, SURROUNDED BY MILLIONS
OF THE MOST VICIOUS CREATURES
ON THE PLANET. HUMANS."

-NEWT SCAMANDER

BOWTRUCKLE

Many species in the animal kingdom mimic other species. Few do it as well as the Bowtruckle. This tiny, thin creature camouflages itself into the trees it inhabits. Green roots splay from a stemlike body for legs and feet, while woody arms and fingers curve out like miniature branches on a tree. Each Bowtruckle looks different from its fellows, with different arrangements of leaves and branches.

Newt planted a small bamboo forest for the Bowtruckle community he saved, and whenever he visits, these little chatterboxes rush out to welcome him.

"TITUS. FINN. JEREMY. ALL PRESENT."

–NEWT SCAMANDER TO THE BOWTRUCKLES

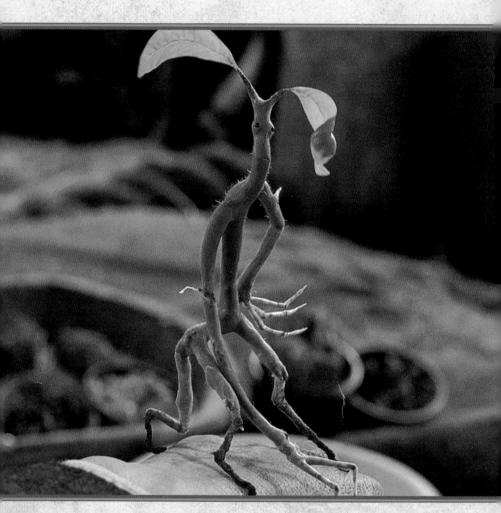

Unlike the other Bowtruckles, Pickett prefers to reside in Newt's greatcoat rather than the bamboo forest. Recently, Pickett had an excuse to do so—he had been ill with a cold and needed Newt's body heat to get well. Now Pickett has grown attached to the warm and friendly Newt, and does not want to go back into the case. Pickett's brothers are jealous and accuse Newt of favoritism, but despite Newt's pleas, Pickett clings to him.

The anxious little Bowtruckle proves himself very helpful when Newt finds himself imprisoned by wizarding authorities inside MACUSA, the Magical Congress of the United States of America.

Pickett comes to the rescue when he inserts his twig-like appendages into the keyhole of Newt's handcuffs, successfully picking the lock and helping Newt escape MACUSA executioners.

DEMIGUISE

To spot a Demiguise in the flesh is to see one of the rarest magical creatures. It is a gangly, apelike beast who is mostly peaceful, but can give a nasty nip if provoked, as the scar on Newt's thumb shows. Its long, silver-white hair and doleful brown eyes give it the appearance of an old, wise sage. This resemblance fits its abilities, for the Demiguise has an incredible power of precognition—an uncanny foresight of predicting the most likely events that will occur in the immediate future. This means that a Demiguise could dodge a pursuer before that pursuer has even given chase!

Trying to catch a Demiguise seems even more futile since it can become invisible. Given these talents, it's a wonder that anyone ever spotted a Demiguise in the first place.

"DEMIGUISE ARE FUNDAMENTALLY PEACEFUL, BUT THEY CAN GIVE A NASTY NIP IF PROVOKED."

—NEWT SCAMANDER

One of Newt's greatest feats could be catching Dougal, a Demiguise, when he escapes from his leather case and turns up in a department store.

To catch a beast who thrives on knowing the presumable outcome of many different future scenarios, Newt has to do the unexpected— act *unpredictably*.

"NO, NO, NO—DOUGAL'S GOT OUT! HIS ARM HAD ONLY JUST HEALED AS WELL!"

—NEWT SCAMANDER

Dougal is a mischievous creature with a sweet tooth, stealing candy when the opportunity arises. Of course, this is not a difficult task for an invisible beast!

Dougal has a softer side as well. He tenderly babysat Newt's young Occamy from the time it was just an egg.

DOXY

The Doxy resembles a chameleon, with bulbous compound eyes that can see in multiple directions at once, and the scaly skin of a lizard that changes colors to fit mood or environment. Long, multicolored ears fan out from its head, giving it exceptional hearing ability.

Not wanting to admit that his fantastic beasts are on the loose all over New York City, Newt dismisses the Doxy that flies past as nothing more than a moth. But Newt's companion, Tina Goldstein, is a former Auror with MACUSA, and is not so easily tricked.

"IT DIDN'T LOOK
LIKE A MOTH."

–TINA GOLDSTEIN

ERUMPENT

The massive Erumpent can be a temperamental beast. Most times, it has a placid, calm nature. It eats several times its own weight in grasses on the plains—resulting in dung that can be the size of boulders! When a female Erumpent is in heat, her mating instincts can transform her into a dangerous aggressor. In such a state, she is virtually impossible to stop.

The Erumpent's dark, blubbery hide protects it from most attacks, while the horn that protrudes from its armored head can be used as a deadly weapon. When its head changes color, the Erumpent is ready for action.

"TELL ME: WHERE DO YOU THINK A—
A MEDIUM-SIZED CREATURE THAT
LIKES BROAD, OPEN PLAINS—
WATERHOLE—TREES—WOULD GO?"

–NEWT SCAMANDER

One of the largest beasts that escapes from the case is a female Erumpent. In heat and searching for a mate, the Erumpent rams through an apartment wall and out into the New York City streets.

Newt and Jacob track down the Erumpent to the Central Park Zoo, where she has trampled fences and cages, releasing many of the animals. Newt gives Jacob special protective clothing as a precaution.

In an effort to catch her attention, Newt dabs a bit of Erumpent musk onto his wrists. Jacob accidentally douses himself in the scent.

The beast gets one whiff of Jacob and charges right at him, her horn brightly glowing. Jacob scrambles up a nearby tree while Newt distracts the Erumpent so that she slides across a sheet of ice—right back into his open case!

FWOOPER

Though small, this birdlike beast can consume giant hunks of meat in one bite. One can only imagine that this heightened ability to swallow may have evolved from necessity due to the competition of larger animals, like the Graphorns.

GRAPHORN

The Graphorn is resistant to domestication, but Newt has successfully won the favor of the last breeding pair in existence. In fact, it's not uncommon for one to place its hooves on the Magizoologist's shoulders and lick his face or hands with its purple tongue. If Newt hadn't saved them, the species would have likely become extinct. But don't be fooled—these same beasts can also savagely rip open a carcass and feast on the meat.

MOONCALF

The Mooncalf is a darling creature with
soft skin, enormous eyes, and webbed feet.
Newt cares for his calves in a special meadow he
has magically created: The meadow gives the
perpetual appearance of a starry night
with the shine of the full moon. Shy at first
encounter, Mooncalves will warm up to
visitors if they have treats.

At Newt's suggestion, Jacob feeds the beasts
special pellets. They sidle up to him, eat from his
hand, and take away all of Jacob's worries and
fears about the unfamiliar magical world.

"WOULD YOU MIND THROWING SOME PELLETS IN WITH THE MOONCALVES? OVER THERE, THE DARK FIELD."

–NEWT SCAMANDER TO JACOB KOWALSKI

MURTLAP

To city dwellers, the
Murtlap might look like an
oversized rat. A mass of tentacles
grows along its back, as if it had
been crossed with a sea anemone.

The Murtlap is most renowned
for its bite. For those of wizarding
blood, the bite can be beneficial,
as it provides momentary
resistance to jinxes and curses. For
No-Majs, however, the bite usually
results in an itchy rash.

Ferocity can sometimes come in small packages—which Jacob Kowalski learns in a sudden and scary confrontation with a Murtlap!

Some No-Majs are more susceptible to a Murtlap's bite, as is the case with Jacob Kowalski. In these worst cases, the reaction to the bite can be very severe: Flames can erupt from the victim's rear end, and a two-day period of uncomfortable itching and twitching can result.

Luckily for Jacob, Newt has a remedy and takes Jacob inside his magical case to get it. Newt gives Jacob tree sap to alleviate the constant itch, and pills to calm his nervous system.

NIFFLER

The beast who proves most troublesome for Newt during his trip to New York is the small, innocuous-looking Niffler. Though it's scarcely larger than a mole, its hunger for shiny things is insatiable. It has beady eyes, dark fur, and a duck-like, flesh-colored bill like a platypus. Oddly, its nose, rather than its eyes, leads the Niffler on its quests. It can sniff out objects that shine and track their luminous scent.

The pouch on its belly is where the Niffler stores its bounty. But the Niffler isn't much of a judge when it comes to appraising an object's worth. As long as it shines—whether it be keys, coins, or even tooth fillings—the Niffler wants it.

"NIFFLER'S GONE, THE LITTLE BUGGER. ANY CHANCE TO GET HIMSELF MORE SHINY STUFF."

-NEWT SCAMANDER

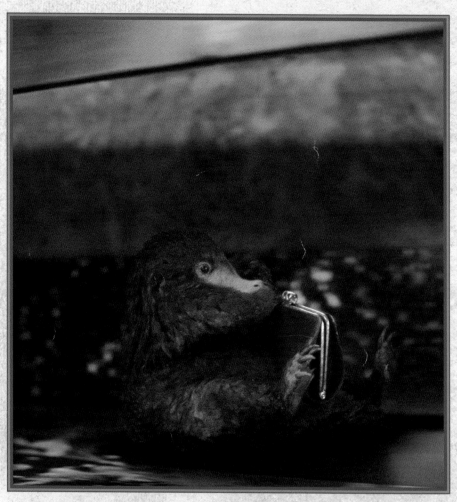

Once the Niffler is out of Newt's case, it squeaks with pleasure as it picks up loose change on the street, digs through pocketbooks, and tries to remove gold buckles from shoes.

The Niffler greedily breaks into the vault at Steen National Bank.

Newt and Jacob chase the Niffler to New York City's Diamond District, where it breaks into a jewelry store. Needless to say, Newt is not pleased with the little pilfering pest—especially when the police think Newt and Jacob are the jewel thieves!

"CALM DOWN, LITTLE ONE. MUMMY'S HERE."
—NEWT SCAMANDER TO AN OCCAMY HATCHLING

OCCAMY

The Occamy is a plumed serpent
with lustrous, iridescent feathers.
Its two large wings are
reminiscent of a dragon, but this
reptile doesn't breathe fire or
eat humans. The Occamy thrives
on a diet of fat worms, and
makes a noise that sounds like
a reverberating hiss.

One innate talent has probably
kept it from extinction up to
this point: The Occamy is
choranaptyxic—it has the power
to change its size to accommodate
a given space. It can enlarge
its body to fill a vast chamber,
or shrink down to fit into a
tiny space.

"HEY, MISTER ENGLISH GUY, I THINK YOUR EGG IS HATCHING!"

–JACOB KOWALSKI

The Occamy's silver eggs fetch a pretty penny on the black market. They are so sought after that there are only a few Occamies left in existence. The creatures have learned to become quite defensive as a result.

The Occamy and its babysitter, Dougal, hide out in a local department store.

Newt devises a plan that plays on the Occamy's choranaptyxic talent and taste for insects. He instructs Tina to capture the beast inside a teapot that contains a cockroach.

It is no easy feat to catch the Demiguise and the Occamy, and the department store is left in shambles.

RUNESPOOR

Bands of bright orange cover the body of the Runespoor and ward off predators who instinctually recognize that a colorful snake is often a venomous one. But it's not necessarily the colorful pattern that induces dread in the Runespoor's victims—it's that this serpent has three heads!

Along with those three heads come three minds of their own. The heads often bicker in disagreement and start fighting each other, making one of the Runespoor's greatest predators *itself*.

The sight of this ferocious beast was terrifying to Jacob, who is petrified of snakes. Despite Newt's mastery of the beast, Jacob maintains a safe distance in the Runespoor's presence.

"THE LOCALS CALL IT SWOOPING EVIL—NOT THE FRIENDLIEST NAME. THEY THOUGHT IT SUCKS OUT BRAINS—BUT IT'S QUITE USEFUL IF YOU'RE IN A FIX."

-NEWT SCAMANDER

SWOOPING EVIL

The Swooping Evil exhibits not only the appearance but also the behaviors of both reptiles and insects. Its reptilian body is spiked and scaly, and its mouth has fierce fangs. These features are coupled with wings that possess the vibrant blue coloration of a moth or butterfly. During periods of dormancy, the Swooping Evil transforms into a spiny cocoon. Newt finds it useful to keep one of these in his pocket.

The Swooping Evil cocoon comes in handy when Newt and Tina are in danger in MACUSA.

Newt tosses the cocoon into the air and the winged beast emerges, giving Newt and Tina a lifesaving getaway ride.

Newt believes the Swooping Evil's venom can be useful, and collects it in a vial for later experimentation. If he can properly dilute it, he thinks the venom could be used to eliminate unwanted memories.

"THAT IS WHY I CAME TO AMERICA.
TO BRING FRANK HOME."

–NEWT SCAMANDER

THUNDERBIRD

The aquiline Thunderbird has six wings
and can arrange its feathers in such a way to
present dazzling pictures of the sun and sky. At
the hint of danger, however, those feathers darken
and lightning illuminates the bird's eyes.
With just a few flaps, the Thunderbird's wings
summon a torrential storm.

The Thunderbird lives in desolate places, like
the deserts of Arizona. The beast carries a price
on its head, and is often sought by hunters.

Newt rescued a Thunderbird he calls "Frank" from a group of poachers. Thanks to Newt, the beast has a second chance at life, and the opportunity to heal.

"I WASN'T GOING TO LEAVE HIM CHAINED."

-NEWT SCAMANDER ON FRANK THE THUNDERBIRD

"I TRY TO LIVE LIKE A BEAST . . .
THEY DON'T FEAR THE END.
THEY CONCENTRATE ON LIVING."

–NEWT SCAMANDER